A New Home for Tiger

A New Home for Tiger

Joan Stimson

Illustrated by

Meg Rutherford

Look out for *Big Panda, Little Panda* also by
Joan Stimson and Meg Rutherford

Scholastic Children's Books,
7-9 Pratt Street, London NW1 0AE, UK
a division of Scholastic Publications Ltd
London ~ New York ~ Toronto ~ Sydney ~ Auckland

First published in the UK by Scholastic Publications Ltd, 1996

Once upon a time there was a cheerful tawny tiger.

He could swim like a fish.
He could eat like a horse.
And each night he slept like a dormouse.

One day at dinner, Mother Tiger
looked excited.
"We're moving, Tiger," she told him.

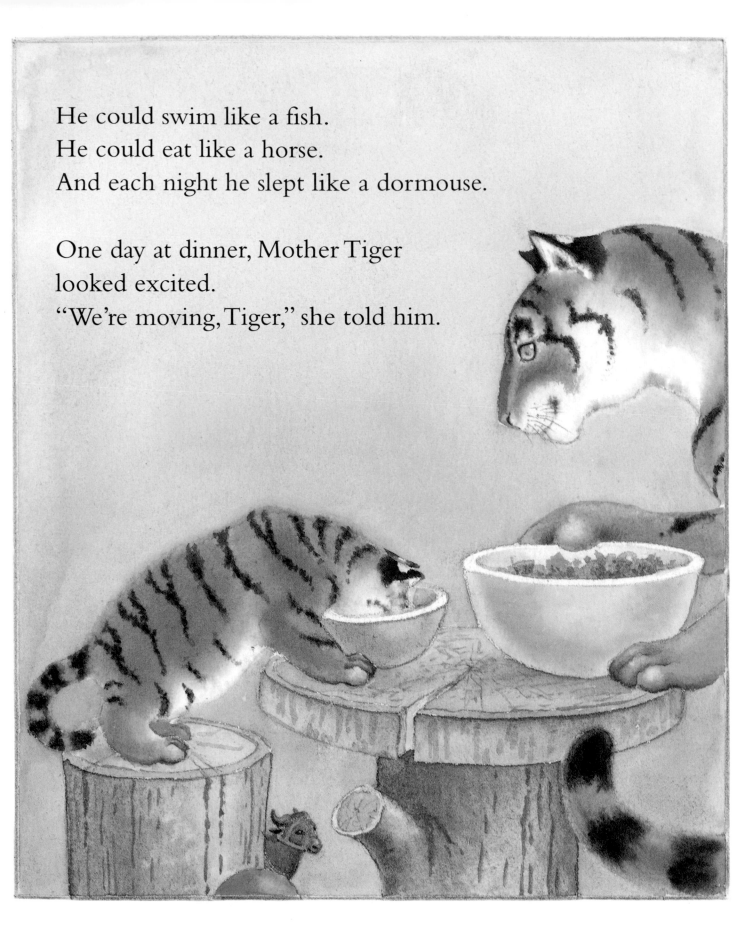

Then she took Tiger outside and pointed across the lake. "I've found a new house for us and tomorrow we must pack up our things."

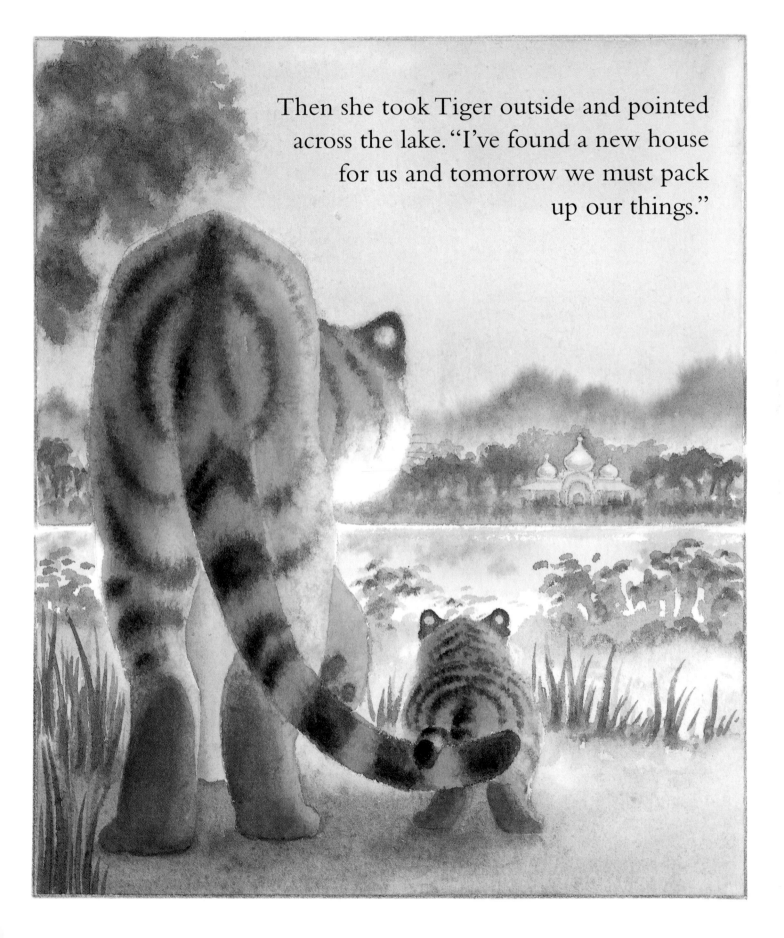

Early next morning Tiger put his toys
in a pile. He bounced round Mum
and helped load the bundles.

"This *is* fun," he said.

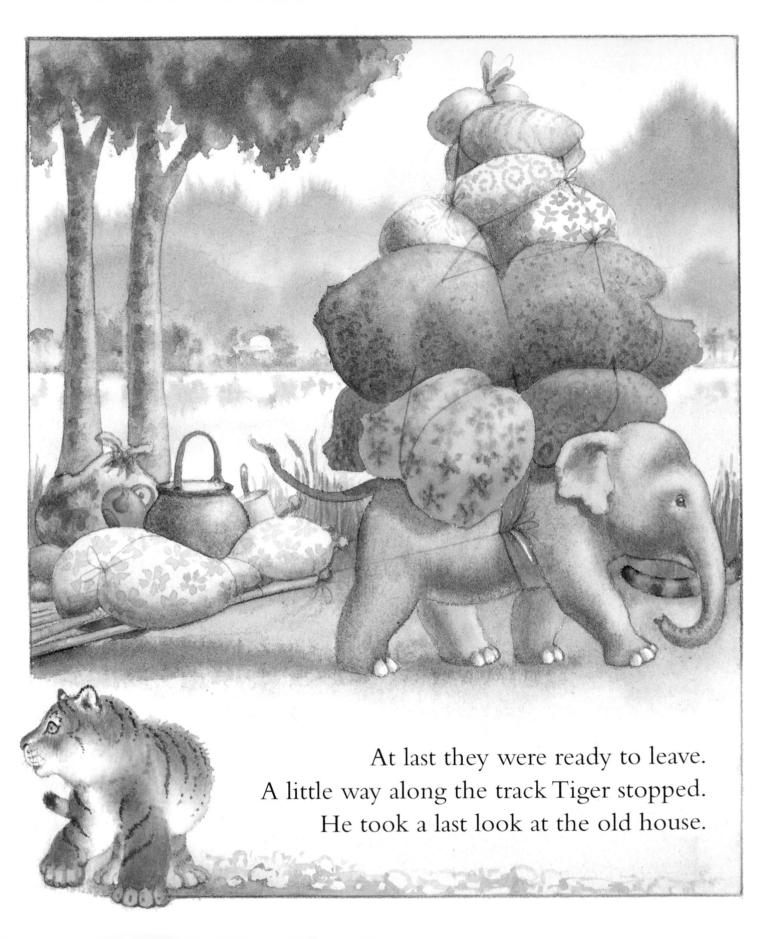

At last they were ready to leave.
A little way along the track Tiger stopped.
He took a last look at the old house.

"Hurry up, Tiger," called Mum, "or we'll never get there."

By the time they reached the new house, it was almost dark.
Tiger padded through the doorway and looked inside.

"It's all different," he whispered after supper. "Can
I sleep in your bed?"
he asked Mum.

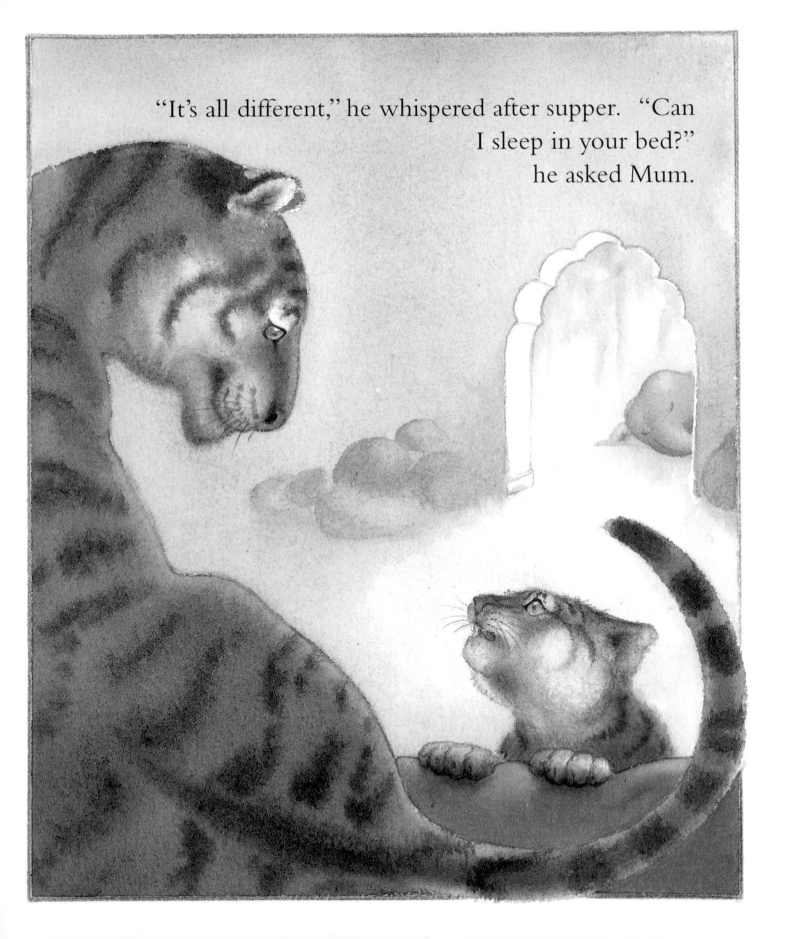

That night Tiger tossed and turned.
When he woke up he wasn't sure
where he was. And, when Mum
began to empty the bundles,
Tiger wouldn't help.

"I don't like it here,"
he wailed.
"I want to go home."

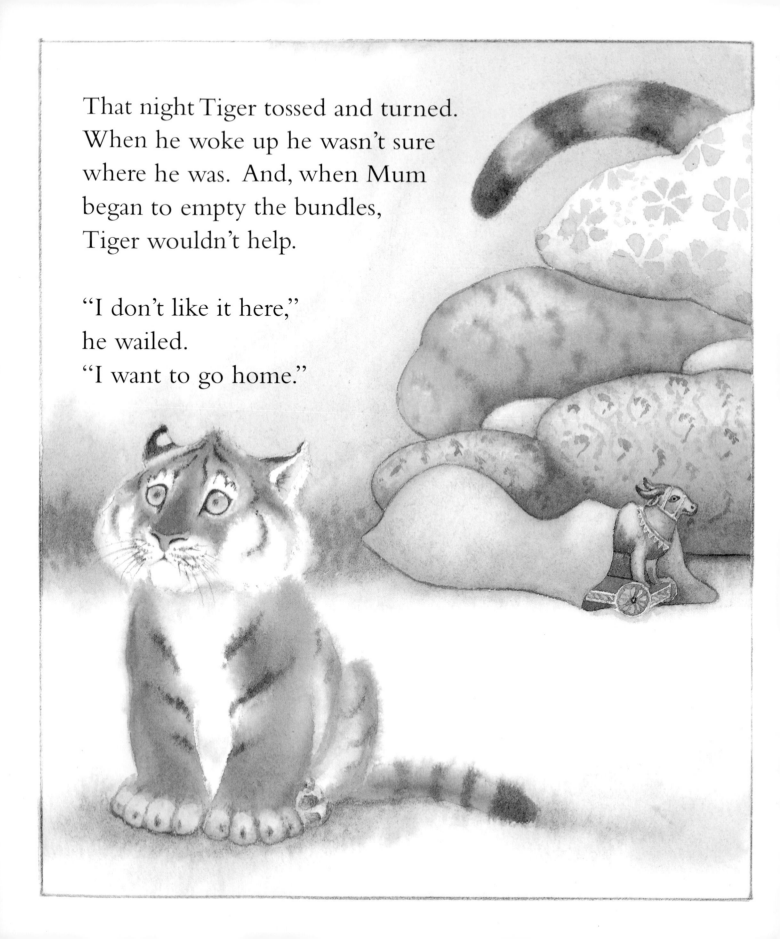

Patiently Mum explained. "We've got a new home now, Tiger." Then she read him his favourite story and gave him a hug.

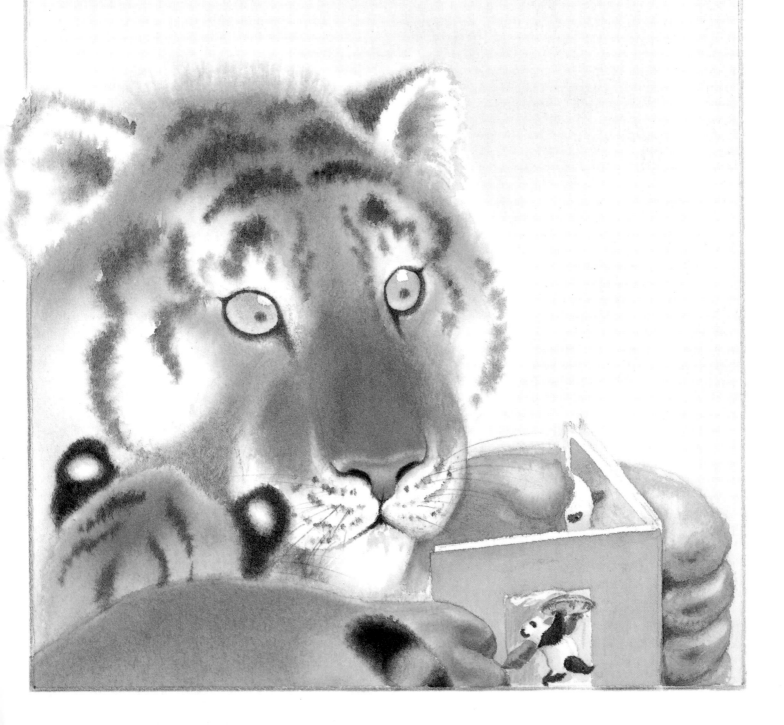

But Tiger still felt grumpy. He refused to swim in the lake with the other tigers. He began to play with his food instead of eating it.

And night after night he woke Mum.
"I want to go home," he kept telling her.

One day Tiger packed up his things.

"I'm going home now," he announced.
"This is our home," explained Mum.

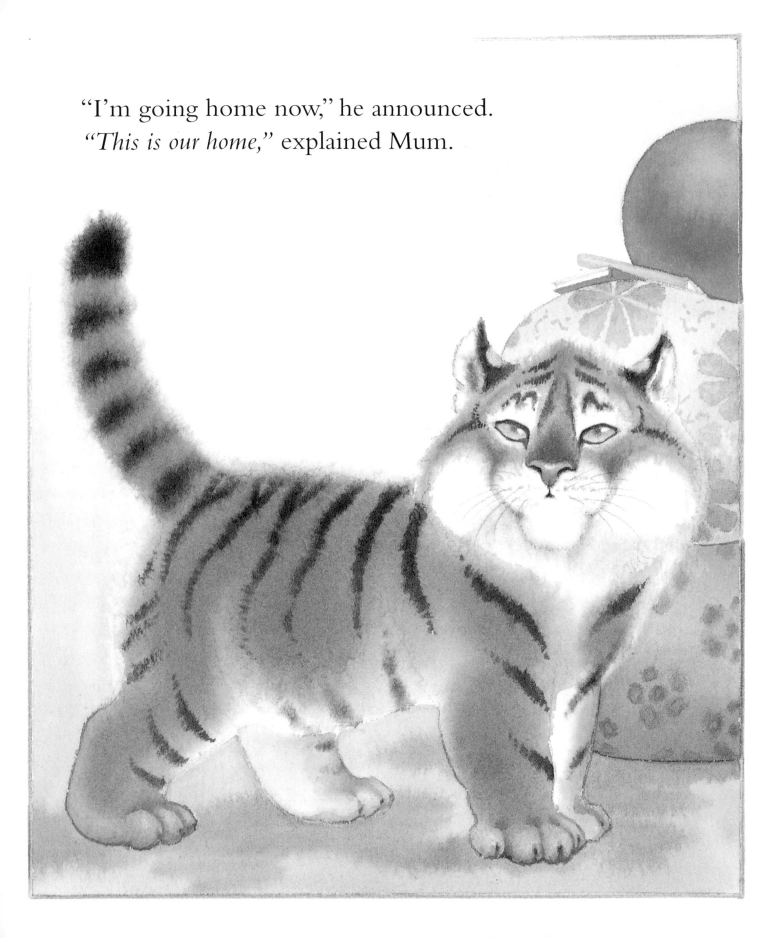

But Tiger had made up his mind.
"If Mum won't take me, then I'll go by myself."

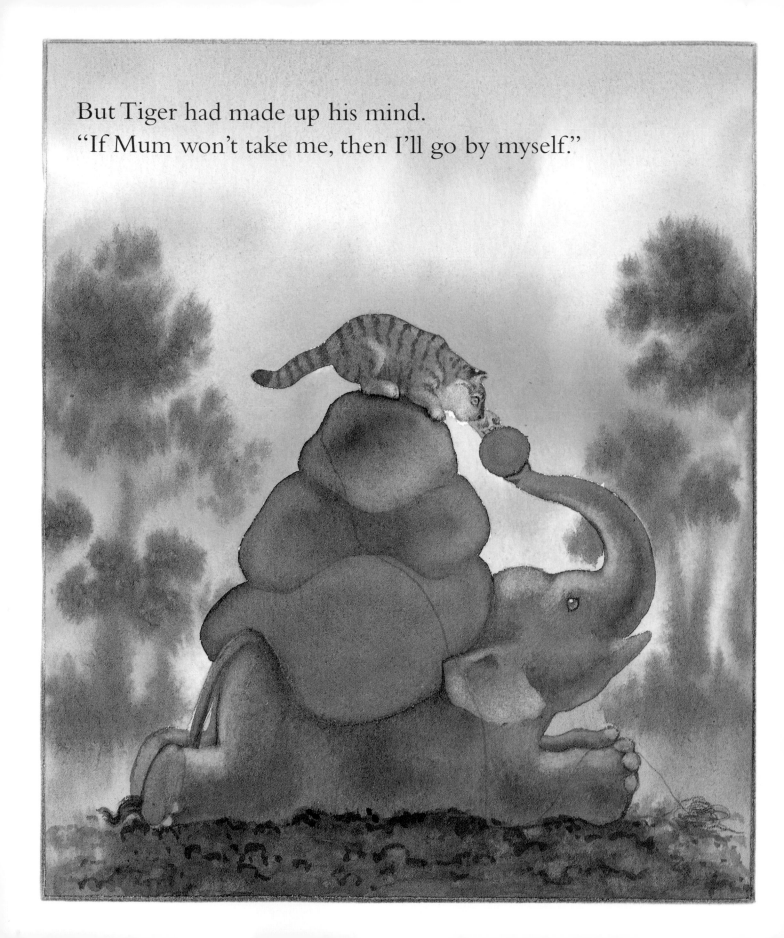

As soon as the moon came up,
Tiger set off.

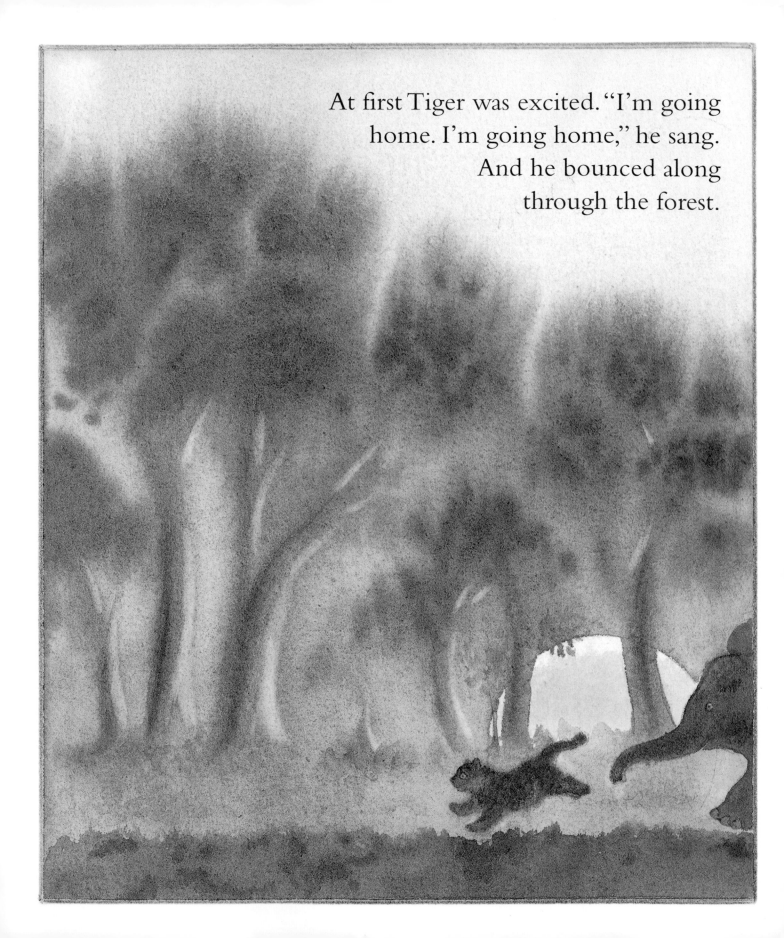

At first Tiger was excited. "I'm going home. I'm going home," he sang. And he bounced along through the forest.

But, when he reached their old
house, the moon disappeared.
Tiger began to feel unsure.
He looked nervously over
his shoulder.

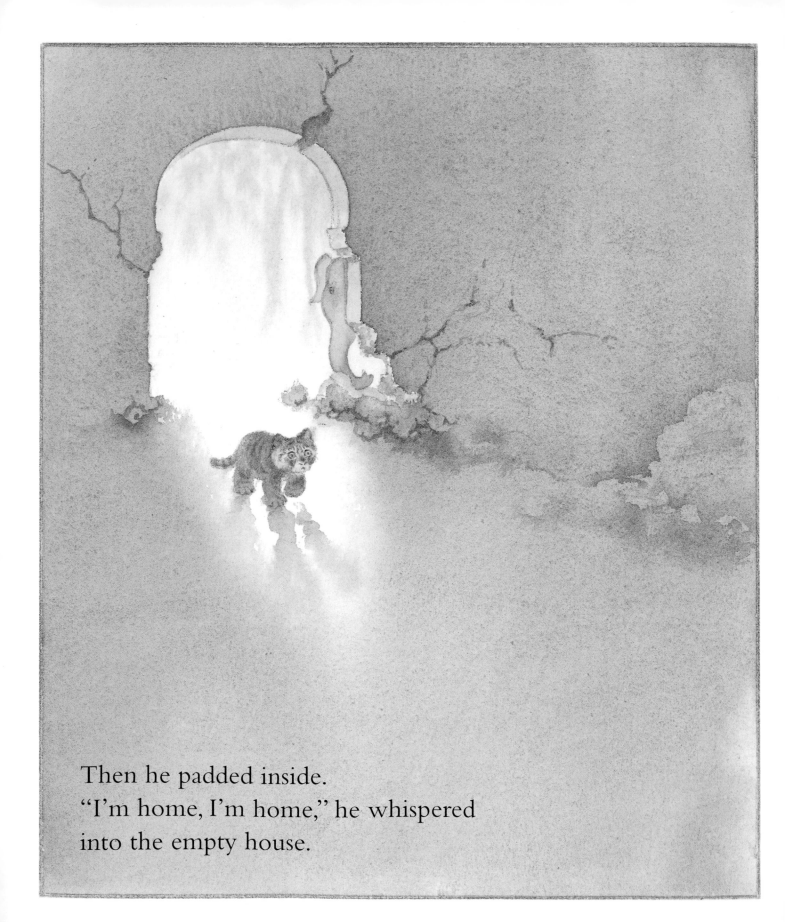

Then he padded inside.
"I'm home, I'm home," he whispered
into the empty house.

But home didn't feel right. There was no sound
of Mum humming or snoring. There was no
smell of her warm fur or a tasty meal.
There was no one to give him a
hug or tell him a story.

Tiger felt confused. Then he realized what was wrong. Tiger bounded all the way back through the forest.

Mother Tiger woke with a start.
"Whatever is it?" she asked.
"I want my home!" cried Tiger. *"I want my home!"*

Mum sat up and yawned. "This is our *new* home..." she began.

But Tiger wouldn't let her finish.

"I know that now!" he cried. Then he tried to explain.
"There's *no* home left in our old house," said Tiger. *"Because
it's all moved here!"*

Next morning a cheerful tawny tiger went out
to play. He splashed in the lake with his new friends.
"Come to dinner at my house," he told them.

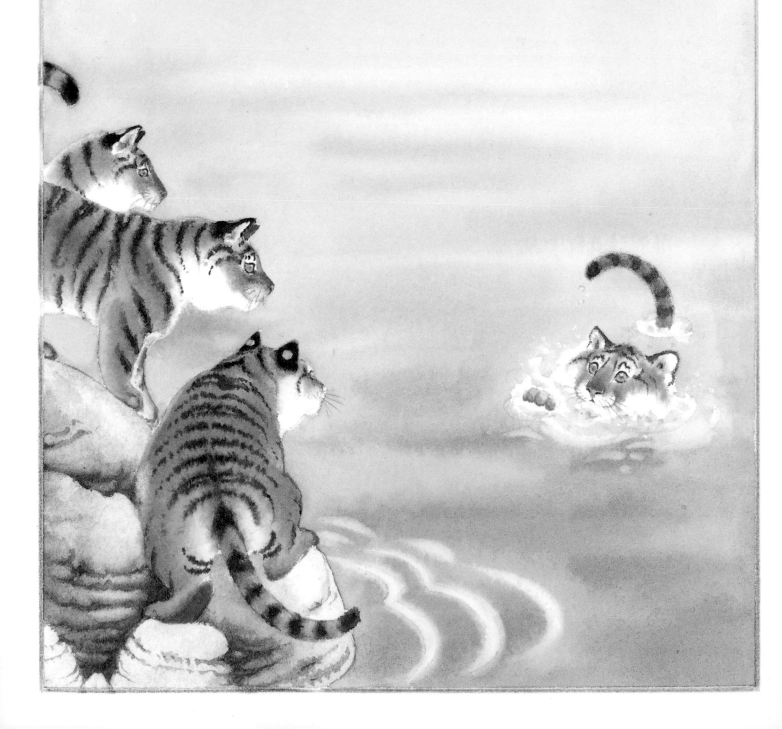